Fish Don't Play Ball

Emma McCann

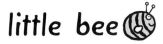

Bob was just dozing off to sleep when Sam burst in with something LARGE and INTERESTING.

"Look Bob!" Said Sam,
very excited.

"Dad bought me a
goldfish! Isn't it great?
It's called Fish."

Bob stared
at Fish.

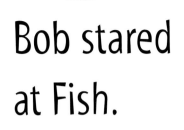

Fish stared
at Bob.

It didn't look great to Bob.
It looked a bit…

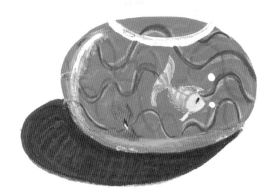

…well, not much fun, actually.

Bob decided he'd come back later when
Fish was doing something
more interesting…

... like juggling,
or something.

Bob watched
Fish from under
the table.

He watched Fish
from behind the
curtains.

He even watched Fish from the garden *(and it was raining too!)*

Obviously, Fish just didn't know what to do.

(Bob decided to help…)

"Perhaps Fish would like to play ball with me," thought Bob. Bob tried very hard to play ball with Fish...

... but Fish just wasn't very good at it.

The ball just floated on top of the water.
Fish wouldn't throw it back.

Sam told Bob off for playing ball with Fish.
"Fish don't play ball, Bob," he said.

"Go back to your basket!"

Sam told him off again when he tried
to share his blanket with Fish…

…and again when he thought
Fish might like a pat on the head.

"Maybe Fish would like to go for a walk," thought Bob.

But when Sam saw Bob drop his lead into Fish's bowl, he got cross.

"Fish don't go for walks, Bob", he said, waggling his finger.

"Go back to your basket!"

Bob loved his basket, but he didn't like being *sent* there.
"Fish aren't very exciting," thought Bob.
"They don't like any of the things I like doing."

Bob lay in his basket and thought very hard about things.

"Fish don't like blankets,
 or being stroked.

"Fish don't do juggling either.

"But worst of all,
 fish don't play ball!"

Sam came in with a little blue pot.
Bob watched as Sam opened it and shook
some funny flaky stuff into Fish's bowl.

Fish started to eat it.

"Humpf," thought Bob.
"At least, I suppose, we both like eating."

"Maybe fish aren't so bad after all…"

For Bonnin
With many thanks to Colin and Jake

E.M.

First published in 2004 by Meadowside Children's Books
185 Fleet Street, London EC4A 2HS
This edition published in 2006 by Little Bee,
an imprint of Meadowside Children's Books

Text and illustrations © Emma McCann 2004

The right of Emma McCann to be identified
as the author and illustrator of this work has been asserted by
her in accordance with the Copyright, Designs and Patents Act, 1988.

A CIP catalogue record for this book is available
from the British Library.
Printed in Thailand

10 9 8 7 6 5 4 3 2